Sudden Drop
published in 2007 by
Hardie Grant Egmont
85 High Street
Prahran, Victoria 3181, Australia
www.hardiegrantegmont.com.au

Hardie Grant Egmont uses
Greenhouse Friendly™
ENVI Carbon Neutral Paper

CONSUMER ENVI Carbon Neutral Paper is an Australian Government
certified Greenhouse Friendly™ Product.

The text for this book has been printed on ENVI Carbon Neutral Paper.

A CiP record for this title is available from the National Library of Australia

Text copyright © 2007 H.I. Larry
Illustration and design copyright © 2007 Hardie Grant Egmont

Cover by Andy Hook
Illustrations by Ben O'Hagan
Based on original illustration and design by Ash Oswald
Typeset by Pauline Haas and Harry von Goes

Printed in Australia by McPherson's Printing Group

11 13 15 14 12

ZAC POWER

24 HOURS TO SAVE THE WORLD ... AND CLEAN THE BATHROOOM

SUDDEN DROP

BY H. I. LARRY

ILLUSTRATIONS BY
BEN O'HAGAN

hardie grant EGMONT

CHAPTER... ...ONE

The thought of his favourite pizza – a large Mexicana, with spicy beef, sour cream and corn chips on top – was the only thing that had kept Zac going all week.

It had been Maths Fun Week at Zac's school. The whole thing was Mrs Tran's idea. Zac's teacher thought that by adding the word 'fun' in between 'maths' and 'week', no-one would notice just how boring and exhausting it really was. Obviously, she was wrong.

Finally it was the weekend, and after guitar practice on Saturday morning Zac took off to the beach for a surf. By lunchtime he was totally starving. He changed out of his wetsuit and into dry clothes. He lugged his surfboard down the pier and got a table outside Mama's Pizza Palace.

When the food finally arrived, Zac breathed in the delicious smell rising from his pizza. But before he could take a single yummy nibble –

SQUAAAAAAAAAAAAAWK!

Feathers flew in all directions! Wings flapped in his face! A huge seagull had landed squarely on Zac's pizza. His spicy beef Mexicana was ruined.

The seagull, with no fear, began pecking at the corn chips! Zac tried to shoo the bird away. He waved his arms and hissed at it, but the beaked bandit wouldn't budge. It marched back and forth across the pizza, stringy cheese caught on its claws.

I don't remember ordering seagull *topping on my pizza!* thought Zac, devastated.

That's when Zac spotted a small, shining disc attached to the seagull's leg. Zac knew exactly what it was – a SpyPad disc!

Zac's mind ticked over. This must be a GIB-trained delivery bird – that's why it wouldn't move from his pizza! The disc

probably contained information about Zac's next mission.

He quickly looked around to check that no-one was watching. Then he reached forward and slipped the disc off the seagull's leg. A good spy would *never* be spotted receiving a secret message.

Nobody knew about Zac Power's secret double life as a spy — except his family. His mum, dad and big brother were all spies, too. They worked for the Government Investigation Bureau, or GIB for short.

All GIB agents were required to carry their SpyPad Turbo Deluxe 3000 wherever they went – even surfing! It's disguised as an ordinary hand-held computer game but is actually a powerful computer, long-range satellite phone, laser, poison detector, video recorder … and that's just for starters. SpyPads have heaps of other unbelievably cool functions.

Zac picked up his gear and left the bird to tuck into his Mexicana pizza. He asked Mama if he could stash his surfboard and wetsuit in her storeroom. He jogged off back down the pier, slotting the disc into his SpyPad.

No pizza, and no more Saturday surf. It was time to get to work!

CHAPTER... ...TWO

'Agent Rock Star!' a familiar voice called out, using Zac's GIB codename.

An awesome-looking powerboat roared alongside the pier, pulling up next to him. 'Ocean Arrow' was painted along one side. GIB Agent Hawk poked his head through the sunroof.

'Oh. Hi, Ned,' said Zac, not at all surprised to see another 12-year-old driving a powerboat.

OCEAN ARROW POWERBOAT

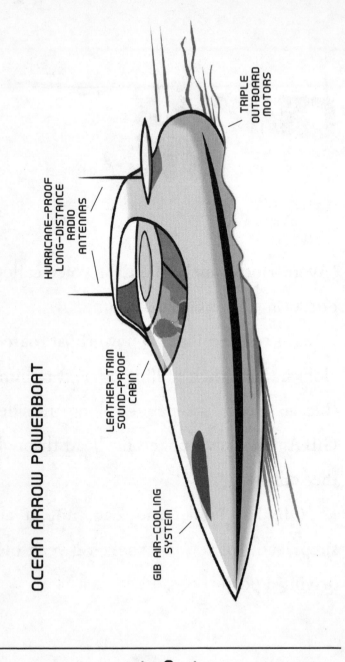

HURRICANE-PROOF
LONG-DISTANCE
RADIO
ANTENNAS

TRIPLE
OUTBOARD
MOTORS

LEATHER-TRIM
SOUND-PROOF
CABIN

GIB AIR-COOLING
SYSTEM

'Climb aboard, quick!' said Agent Hawk, signalling to Zac.

Ned was a fellow GIB spy who Zac knew from training. He was a really good agent. In fact, Ned was always competing with Zac for the top spot on the GIB Spy Ladder. But Zac was still on the top.

'Sounds serious,' said Zac, checking out the Ocean Arrow cruiser.

'Get in and read your mission info disc,' said Agent Hawk, urgently. 'It'll become clearer then.'

Zac settled into the passenger seat of the sleek powerboat and fired up his SpyPad. Vital details from GIB headquarters filled the screen.

■ ■ ■ ■ ■ ■ ■ ■

CLASSIFIED
FOR THE EYES OF ZAC POWER ONLY

MESSAGE RECEIVED
SATURDAY 12.09PM

Government geologists have discovered a
hidden lake inside Craggy Mountain.
It contains enough water to supply the
entire country. Pipes have been laid and
pumping was set to begin immediately.

But now the millions of gigalitres of water
are in danger – enemy spy agency BIG has
taken over the pumping station and
planted explosives. They are holding
the water to ransom!

URGENT INSTRUCTIONS

• Proceed immediately to GIB's Aqua Glide
Bullet-Cat. You will be briefed on your
mission upon arrival.

END

   MEXICANA PIZZA MODE
>>> OFF

The country was in the grip of the worst drought in history. The government urgently needed these fresh water supplies – every man, woman and child was depending on it. Enemy spy organisation BIG were ruthless and cunning. Zac had faced them on previous missions.

'Sounds bad, right?' said Ned. 'We always knew that BIG would take advantage of worldwide climate change as soon as they got the chance. They're demanding to be paid nine *billion* dollars ransom by midday tomorrow! If the money doesn't show, they're going to dynamite the Craggy Mountain pumping station and allow all the water to flood out.'

'No time to waste,' said Zac, buckling up his seat belt. 'Let's see what this powerboat can do!'

Beneath them, the triple outboard motors roared like an angry sea beast. The Ocean Arrow shot forward, and Zac and Ned were thrown back into their seats at a G-force of about 5.5. Within seconds, Mama's was just a speck on the horizon behind them.

The two GIB spies sped across the waves of the open sea. With its dark blue paint job, the Ocean Arrow matched the water around it. The awesome cruiser was perfectly camouflaged as it skimmed the surface of the water.

Zac and Ned were protected from spray and noise by the luxurious, sound-proof cabin. The Ocean Arrow was rock steady even at ultra-high speed. Twin fins jutted from either side, allowing the vessel to slice through jumbo waves.

'Sweet ride!' said Zac, grinning. He got comfortable in the plush seats, hands behind his head.

'This is just the baby sister of the main ship,' explained Agent Hawk. 'Wait until you see GIB's Aqua Glide Bullet-Cat – it's hot! My orders are to deliver you there without delay...you know it really is no fun being number two on the Spy Ladder, Zac. All I get are these jobs as your water-taxi!'

Zac was curious. 'What do *you* know about this mission?' he asked Ned.

'Not much,' said Agent Hawk. 'The Aqua Glide is anchored at the mouth of the Gecko River. It's the only waterway that flows anywhere near Craggy Mountain. You're going to be briefed on board so that we can head up-river while you're given the latest confidential reports and special mission equipment.'

Excellent, thought Zac. *That means I'm getting some new gadgets!*

'Any other insider information you can tell me?' quizzed Zac, excitedly.

'Oh, yeah. Mission Control received a coded message for you from Agent Tool

Belt,' said Agent Hawk, eyeing off the clock on the Ocean Arrow's dashboard. 'It said "ZP ON BD@16:30 SUN". Do you know what that means?'

'Great,' mumbled Zac, slouching back into his seat. 'That's a message from my dad. I'm on bathroom duty tomorrow — mopping, scrubbing and toilet cleaning!'

CHAPTER... ...THREE

It was late in the afternoon by the time they spotted the Aqua Glide Bullet-Cat.

The Aqua Glide was just as cool as Ned had said. It was a huge, triple-hulled, high-performance catamaran. It was hard to spot as it was painted the same camouflaged dark blue as the Ocean Arrow.

Agent Hawk steered the smaller cruiser into the Aqua Glide's docking bay.

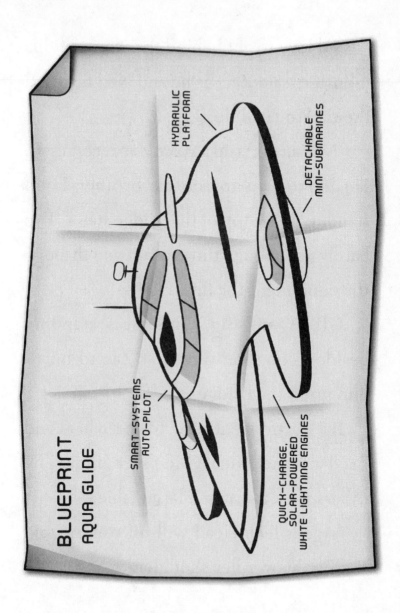

BLUEPRINT
AQUA GLIDE

HYDRAULIC PLATFORM

DETACHABLE MINI-SUBMARINES

SMART-SYSTEMS AUTO-PILOT

QUICK-CHARGE, SOLAR-POWERED WHITE LIGHTNING ENGINES

'I'd love to get behind the wheel of this monster,' said Zac, as he and Ned boarded the the Aqua Glide.

'No can do,' said a voice Zac recognised. He looked up to see his brother Leon standing at the top of the bridge stairs. 'I've barely got enough time to run you through the equipment for this mission!'

GIB Agent Big Turtle was standing beside Leon. She waved at Zac to hurry him up to the bridge.

Big Turtle went over to the wheel and fired up the Aqua Glide's engines. The others took a seat at a large table.

'Agent Tech Head will fill you in,' said Big Turtle over her shoulder.

With a powerful rumbling, the Aqua Glide quickly moved off, heading up the Gecko River. Zac looked at his watch. They really had to get the ship closer to his target – and fast.

The GIB agents got down to business.

'Zac, this mission is extremely dangerous and of utmost importance,' said Leon. 'We must secure that water. Let me explain: thousands of years ago, Craggy

Mountain was an extinct volcano covered with a layer of snow almost half a kilometre thick. When the Earth warmed, the snow melted. Pure, clean water drained down and was trapped inside Craggy Mountain's hollow crater.

'So, that dead volcano is now the biggest natural water tank on the planet?' said Zac, thinking aloud.

'Yes, and BIG control the pumping station on top of the hidden lake,' continued Leon. 'If they don't get the money they want – boom! Your mission is to make sure BIG don't dynamite the pumping station, and to get that water flowing to our cities right away.'

Leon paused and waited for Zac's reaction. Leon could be a bit of a nerd but he took his GIB job very seriously.

'I get you loud and clear,' said Zac. 'But how am I going to deliver nine billion dollars in cash to BIG in time?'

'There's no ransom,' said Leon. 'GIB does *not* negotiate. It's up to you to regain control of the pumping station, Zac.'

'Enough chatting,' interrupted Agent Big Turtle. 'Let's go over your transport.'

She had put the Aqua Glide on auto-pilot and pressed an orange switch to her right. They all made their way to the forward deck of the Aqua Glide.

They had just stepped outside when

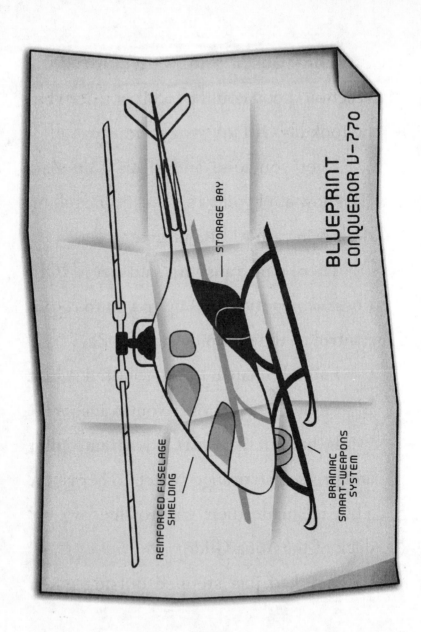

BLUEPRINT
CONQUEROR U-770

REINFORCED FUSELAGE
SHIELDING

STORAGE BAY

BRAINIAC
SMART-WEAPONS
SYSTEM

huge sliding doors in the floor of the deck started to part. In seconds, a hydraulic platform rose up from inside the Bullet-Cat's hull. On it stood a mind-blowing helicopter.

'The Conqueror V-770,' said Leon, tossing Zac a set of keys. 'It's fully loaded — just needs an ace pilot.'

The chopper was painted with a bush camouflage pattern. High-visibility cockpit glass sparkled in the late afternoon sun.

'Unfortunately, the Conqueror isn't small enough to land on Craggy Mountain,' said Leon. 'You'll have to swap to the Trek Titan 4WD for the final part of your journey. You'll find it in the helicopter's storage bay.'

Leon looked at Zac. 'BIG have blocked the main entrance to the pumping station at ground level and have all the smaller emergency exits heavily guarded and booby trapped. The only way to get into the mountain is from the top. The mountain climb will be extremely tough,' he said seriously. 'We're really throwing you in at the deep end, Zac.'

'That's OK,' said Zac with a wink. 'The deep end is where I do my best swimming.'

CHAPTER... ...FOUR

Leon went over his checklist one more time, running through Zac's special mission equipment.

'Ah, yes, the Fizzle-44 Explosion Inhibitor,' said Leon, handing Zac a gadget that looked like a car alarm activator.

'It's small and easy to use,' Leon continued. 'It'll take the bang out of BIG's bombs. Attach it to one bomb and it will detect and defuse all others in the area.'

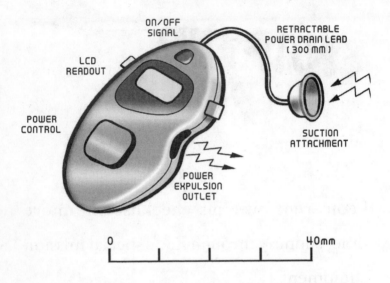

FIZZLE-44 EXPLOSION INHIBITOR

ON/OFF SIGNAL

LCD READOUT

RETRACTABLE POWER DRAIN LEAD (300 mm)

POWER CONTROL

SUCTION ATTACHMENT

POWER EXPULSION OUTLET

0   40mm

Zac quickly pocketed the new gadget.

'The whole Craggy Mountain area will be heavily guarded with the latest BIG weaponry,' continued Leon. 'So this could come in very handy.'

He reached into the Conqueror and took out what looked like a ray gun. Smooth, curved, with a pistol grip and shoulder strap.

'I call it the BOPS – Black-Out Power Sucker,' said Leon. 'It completely drains the energy from machinery and electronic equipment. But it only has a temporary effect, so whatever you zap will return to normal in a few hours. Oh, and it doesn't

BLACK-OUT POWER SUCKER (BOPS)

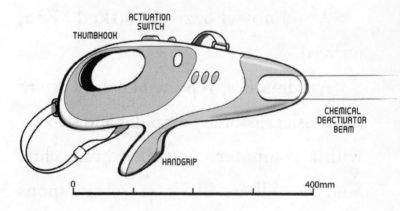

ACTIVATION SWITCH

THUMBHOOK

CHEMICAL DEACTIVATOR BEAM

HANDGRIP

0   400mm

work on humans – otherwise you could just leave those BIG agents snoring and hand-cuffed!'

'Leon,' Agent Big Turtle said, butting in, 'it's no use putting it off. You'll have to tell Zac about the creatures.'

'I was saving the worst news for last,' said Leon, sounding nervous. 'Zac, you'll probably come up against some Arachnotiles.'

'Arachno-whozzits?' asked Zac, puzzled.

'Arachnotiles,' repeated Leon. 'They're a freakish crossbreed of spider and snake – with a computer-controlled brain chip. Sources tell us BIG's secret weapons laboratory have been working overtime to develop them. They're vicious, venomous, mutant predators. A bite or scratch from an Arachnotile is fatal in seconds.'

'They have the body of a snake and the legs and fangs of a spider,' added Agent Big Turtle. 'And eight beady snake eyes that swivel in all directions.'

Zac shuddered at the thought of coming across an Arachnotile in the dark.

Zac checked his watch.

'All right. Well, I'd better get moving then,' he said.

Zac hoisted himself into the Conqueror V-770's cockpit. 'Mmmm, I love that new helicopter smell,' he smiled to himself.

He pulled on the helmet from the seat beside him and gave the other GIB agents the thumbs up.

'It's rugged territory you're headed into Zac...be careful,' said Agent Big Turtle.

Zac did a quick pre-flight check and hit the starter button. The rotor blades began to turn. Zac had trained on most

GIB aircraft, so the Conqueror V-770 was just as easy for him to use as his iPod.

With the engines warmed up Zac cranked the throttle. The chopper lifted off the Bullet-Cat's deck and rose into the air. The GPS on the control panel blinked on. Leon had programmed in directions to Craggy Mountain.

My brother can be a geek but he does take care of me, Zac thought to himself.

He nudged the joystick forward, sending the helicopter hurtling off.

CHAPTER... ...FIVE

Zac bought the speeding helicopter down closer to the surface of the Gecko River. It was good to be in the air after taking in so many mission details.

Barely skimming the water, Zac took the chance to test out the Conqueror. He soared and dived through narrow, rocky outcrops. He swooped out over the rippling grasslands beside the water.

The kilometres whipped by underneath Zac. Shrivelled by drought, the Gecko River soon became a shallow creek.

After another hour of flying, the creek had totally dried up. Zac found himself flying over kilometres of cracked earth.

Just as the sun was beginning to set, Zac spotted Craggy Mountain. It looked like an enormous castle of red rock. Zac thought it was amazing that there could be water hidden anywhere out here.

The wildlife had almost all disappeared, too — except for a flock of amazingly coloured parrots. They were a dazzling green, red, yellow…and silver?!

Zac's spy senses tingled. Something wasn't right.

Zac checked his speedometer. The Conqueror was flying at 215 knots, which is almost 400 kilometres an hour — and the birds were keeping up!

With his free hand Zac took out his SpyPad. He held it up to the cockpit glass and pointed it at the nearest parrot. The SpyPad locked on and scanned the bird. Within seconds, the SpyPad had loaded up the information.

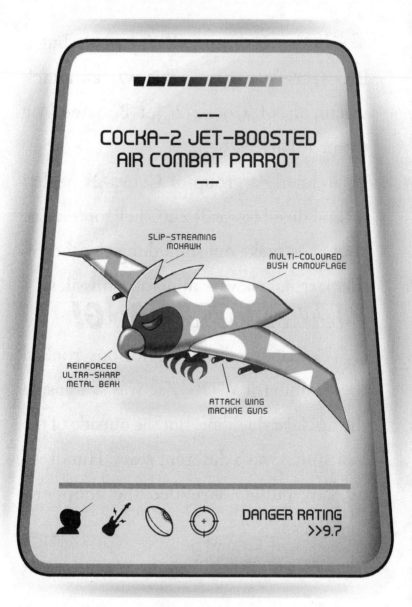

COCKA-2 JET-BOOSTED
AIR COMBAT PARROT

SLIP-STREAMING
MOHAWK

MULTI-COLOURED
BUSH CAMOUFLAGE

REINFORCED
ULTRA-SHARP
METAL BEAK

ATTACK WING
MACHINE GUNS

DANGER RATING
>>9.7

These were no ordinary birds but a BIG secret weapon — this was an attack squadron of Cocka-2 Jet-Boosted Air Combat Parrots!

Suddenly a group of Cocka-2s peeled off and dived towards Zac's helicopter. Zac could just make out something clutched in the parrots' claws — miniature missiles.

KAAABOOM! BANG!

The bangs of tiny explosions rocked the Conqueror V-770. Zac was safe inside the fuselage shielding. But the outside of the helicopter was a different story. Hundreds of baby bullets shredded the chopper's fuel lines.

First a pizza-squishing seagull, now

psycho robot parrots — birds were ruining Zac's day!

Zac was really in trouble. *What can I do?* he asked himself. Then he remembered the chopper's Brainiac Smart-Weapons system.

He pushed the activation button and the Brainiac started processing.

Let's see what this system can do, thought Zac.

The Braniac system beeped loudly as it calculated what to do. Then suddenly there was a bright light as an emergency distress flare fired from underneath the chopper. It burned and fizzled as it flew… and then spluttered and smoked as it fell to the ground!

Zac had hoped for something with a little more stopping power.

But for a moment the attack seemed to have stopped. Zac looked around. Strangely, not as many Cocka-2s were trailing behind him. Most of the swarm had powered off to chase the distress flare.

The smart-weapons system made a smart decision after all, thought Zac. The birds must be heat-seeking weapons.

Zac smiled to himself. *That gives me an idea!*

He dived towards the rocky earth, levelling off a metre above the ground. Petrol from his damaged fuel lines sprayed over the jagged rocks below. Zac activated the chopper's laser and locked the target onto the puddles of petrol below him.

The laser beam sliced through the air and set alight the spilt fuel on the rocks. Zac twisted the throttle and jerked the joystick back hard, sending him straight upwards. Behind him the petrol exploded in a huge fireball – and Zac just managed to avoid being swallowed up by it!

The Cocka-2s flew straight for the fireball. Those that got too close were burnt to a Cocka-crisp. The rest circled in confusion, firing stupidly into the blaze.

Zac had to get away from the explosion. But the Conqueror wouldn't limp much further. It was getting too dark outside to locate a safe site – he was just going to have to crash land!

Zac had less than a cup of fuel left in his tank when the chopper's landing skids crunched against the ground. He landed with such force that the helicopter's legs buckled and then tore completely loose in a shower of sparks. The Conqueror slid along on its belly and finally came to a stop when it thudded into a dead tree trunk.

As soon as Zac stepped down from the cockpit the crushing heat hit him. It was almost dark but the rocks were still warm from the scorching sun.

The remaining Cocka-2s would come looking for Zac's helicopter again as soon as the fire died down. He had to scram before they found him.

Time to roll out the Trek Titan!

CHAPTER... ...SIX

In the distance, the glow from the fuel fireball was fading into the darkness.

Zac peered up at the murky sky. There were no Cocka-2s in sight.

Zac turned a lever and lowered the helicopter ramp to reveal the Trek Titan 4WD. It was one of GIB's finest vehicle designs yet.

He climbed behind the wheel of the

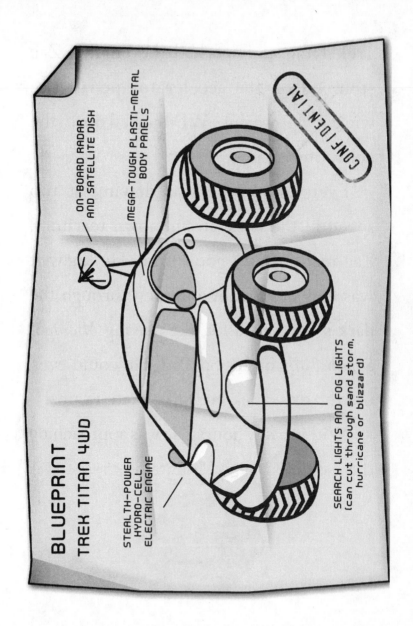

BLUEPRINT
TREK TITAN 4WD

ON-BOARD RADAR
AND SATELLITE DISH

MEGA-TOUGH PLASTI-METAL
BODY PANELS

CONFIDENTIAL

STEALTH-POWER
HYDRO-CELL
ELECTRIC ENGINE

SEARCH LIGHTS AND FOG LIGHTS
(can cut through sand storm,
hurricane or blizzard)

Trek Titan and sparked the engine. Zac stomped on the accelerator pedal. The wickedly powerful 4WD bucked down the helicopter's ramp.

Even though he was driving at top speed in the dark, in unknown territory, Zac made pretty good time. He knew it was dangerous, but zooming through the dark scrub was a lot like playing *Midnight Smash Rally* on his SpyPad. He could even use the dry creek beds like skate ramps!

Within a few hours Zac was approaching the base of Craggy Mountain.

Zac skidded to a stop, sending up a shower of loose rocks. The sheer cliff of the mountain towered above him. It looked like the rest of the trip was going to be straight up.

In the Trek Titan's boot he found a backpack full of GIB-issued extreme climbing gear. He hoisted it over his shoulder, after making sure his iPod and the BOPS were safely stowed inside.

Zac's SpyPad clicked and buzzed as he scanned the mountain. In seconds it displayed the safest climbing route.

He flicked over to X-ray function and locked onto the location of the hidden lake inside the towering mountain.

I'd better get climbing, thought Zac.

Zac fished around in the backpack and pulled out some night-vision goggles and a high-pressure, gas-injected climbing clamp launcher. He took steady aim at the wall of rock and fired.

SHOOOOOOOSH –CLANK!

The clamp sunk into the rock-face 130 metres above him. The climbing rope trailed down to the ground. Zac strapped on an abseiling harness with the built-in power winch. He carefully attached the climbing rope, put on his night-vision goggles and started the winch motor. The rope quickly began to wind in, lifting Zac into the air and up the face of Craggy Mountain.

This is heaps faster than climbing, thought Zac, smiling to himself.

He was soon within arm's reach of his clamp. He got a firm grip on the rock with one hand and with the other hand he reloaded the launcher.

KERCHUNK!

An even better shot. This time Zac scaled 220 metres of sheer rock face in less than 15 minutes! Normally this would have been an eight-hour rock climb!

Halfway up the mountain a strong breeze became a problem. Zac had to slow his ascent, taking care to keep a reliable hand-hold in case the cold wind blew him sideways into the jagged rock.

Zac had a quick look at his watch. His mission time was slipping away and he still hadn't made it to the pumping station.

Zac found a protected ledge in the opening to a small cave. He stopped to rest and escape the icy wind for a few minutes. He pulled off his goggles and pulled on his woollen GIBeanie.

He got out his SpyPad and scanned the area to make certain he was on course.

But what are the three strange, fuzzy squiggles on the SpyPad screen, wondered Zac. *BIG agents?*

They were moving toward him from inside the mountain – fast!

Zac desperately looked around for an escape route, but there was nowhere to go except down.

Zac heard a spine-tingling hiss behind him. He turned around to see dozens of evil, slitted eyes appear in the blackness of the cave. An instant later three hissing Arachnotile mouths emerged – their fangs dripping with venom.

There was nothing else Zac could do. He whipped around and ran straight for the

edge of the ledge. He grabbed the climbing rope and threw himself over the side of the mountain – down into the pitch black!

CHAPTER... ...SEVEN

The wind roared in Zac's ears as he fell in the dark. He had no idea how far he was from the ground, but he knew that he was falling way too fast!

Zac didn't know how much rope he had left, but he surely only had a few seconds to secure the rope somehow before it would be too late. Quickly, he fed the end of the rope into the power winch. It whirred onto the winder. Smoke puffed out from the winch. The little motor screamed, burned out and jammed!

THUUUUUUNK!

The rope was tangled tight in the winch, saving his life. But the sudden drop and stop had swung him far out from the rock-face. Zac knew that he would soon be slammed back against the rock. He got into his crash-landing position just in time to avoid being splattered onto the rock-face.

A hail of stones narrowly missed him. He counted as they fell below him and listened as they shattered far below. Judging from the size of the rocks and how long they took to fall, Zac calculated that he was about 200 metres off the ground. Great! He'd fallen about 150 metres.

He took a few deep breaths and tried to work on a plan.

The Arachnotiles had come *out* of the cave. That meant that the cave must lead back *inside* the mountain to the pumping station – and that was exactly the direction that Zac needed to go.

There was no other choice. Zac had to get back up to that ledge, take on the Arachnotiles and get inside that cave.

The power winch was totally fried from breaking Zac's fall. He realised he was going to have to climb the rest of the mountain the hard way.

Zac grasped onto the mountainside, unclipped his harness and let it fall. The weight would only slow him down.

Silently, Zac began to make his way back up the mountain. The climb was highly dangerous with no support belt. He heaved himself up a few centimetres at a time.

It was taking forever to get back up to the ledge. Daylight was breaking, showing Zac how much further he still had to go.

Cold, hungry and tired, Zac finally

made it back to the rock ledge. Nothing moved above him. The Arachnotiles must have given up and retreated into the cave.

To be on the safe side, Zac reached around and slid the BOPS out of his backpack. He hung the gadget around his neck and hauled himself up on the ledge, rolling forward commando-style.

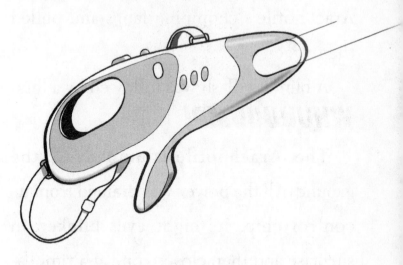

A sudden movement to the left caught his eye. One of the Arachnotiles had been left on guard duty!

The creature lunged at Zac with its mouth wide and fangs bared.

'Hungry, eh?' yelled Zac. 'Then bite on this!'

He crammed the BOPS between the Arachnotile's chomping fangs and pulled the trigger.

A blinding flash was followed by a loud **WHUUUUUMP!**

The Arachnotile slumped to the ground. All the power was drained from its control chip. Its eight eyes blinked in surprise and then closed, one at a time.

It was stunned — alive but unable to move a muscle.

But the BOPS was trashed though. It was gooey with venom that had already started to eat through the gun.

Zac looked down the mouth of the cave. The passage into the mountain was going to be a tight fit. Zac would have to ditch his backpack. He reached inside and fished out his iPod and SpyPad. Then he knelt down and crawled inside.

Zac set his SpyPad to Spotlight so he could shine it into any dark spaces that might hide Arachnotiles.

After hours of being snagged by razor-sharp rocks, and nearly choking on cave dust,

Zac noticed the tunnel widening out. He must be nearing the pumping station now.

In ten minutes he heard trickling, dripping, bubbling and loud sloshing up ahead.

Zac could now stand without scraping his head. He tip-toed forward and peered around the corner.

The cave led straight to a massive, brightly-lit opening inside the mountain – the pumping station!

Zac couldn't risk being spotted now. He set his SpyPad to Video Camera and hit Record. He poked it just outside the lip of the cave.

After swivelling the SpyPad camera left and right Zac checked what he'd recorded.

The gigantic cavern was the size of ten aircraft hangars — and this was just the surface of the lake trapped inside the mountain. Zac knew the water was hundreds of metres deep.

Above the water, the lake was crisscrossed with a network of ramps, platforms and walkways. Hulking BIG guards patrolled the entire area, moving about on the metal walkways.

Huge shiny pipes rose up from the lake. Complicated machinery was fitted into the rock walls. Tunnels led off in all directions to other parts of the pumping station.

On one of the walkways, in the centre of the huge cavern, stood a woman barking orders. Zac immediately recognised the face on his SpyPad screen.

Captain Stewart!

The last time Zac had seen her was on a submarine 2000 feet under water, at the bottom of the West Sea!

CHAPTER... ...EIGHT

Zac had faced Captain Stewart on one of his first ever GIB missions, when he'd destroyed her top-secret Sea Devil submarine. He cringed as he remembered that he'd had to knock Stewart unconscious with a well-aimed iPod to the head. Zac couldn't believe what a newbie he'd been!

BIG had obviously put Captain Stewart to be in charge of this water ransom operation. And Zac had a strong feeling she would *not* be pleased to see him again.

Captain Stewart had a score to settle with Zac. She would definitely be on the lookout for him — as would the army of mean-looking BIG guards!

Zac had to find a way to put the guards out of action or he'd be captured before he could complete the mission.

But what could he do? Zac sat in his hiding spot, racking his brains for a plan. He couldn't think of anything so he pulled out his iPod and started flicking through the menu, hoping to find something to use.

Just then, a shrieking siren echoed in Zac's ears.

An alarm? thought Zac, worried. *Have they spotted me?*

Zac glanced outside the cave, fearing the worst. But Captain Stewart and the guards were walking toward one of the tunnels in the cavern wall. Zac switched his SpyPad to Super-Sensitive Microphone mode and listened.

'I'm starving,' said one of the BIG guards. 'I thought that morning tea siren would never go off!'

'I'm so hungry I could eat *your* socks,' replied another guard. 'I hear we're having omelette surprise. I bet it's just left-overs mixed with eggs again.'

Zac had a brain wave. All the guards would be eating the same meal. If he was quick, he could add a surprise ingredient of his own to their omelette surprise.

Choosing the Poison Detector on his SpyPad, he scanned the walls of the cave around him. Gross moss and slimy plants grew in the moist corners. The SpyPad beeped as a result popped up on the screen.

Zac quietly crawled over and helped himself to a clump of Belly Buster berries.

Also known as the Poopy Pants plant, Zac remembered the name from his days at GIB's Spy Training Academy. If cooked for nine weeks, these berries tasted like chocolate donuts. Cooked for any less than that and they caused crippling stomach pains – and trips to the toilet!

With Zac in the kitchen, morning tea was *not* going to be very pleasant.

Most of the guards were heading hungrily for the canteen. Only four were left behind to protect against intruders.

Zac quickly wrapped the Belly Buster berries in his GIBeanie. He darted from the cave and took cover behind one of the king-sized water pipes.

Zac took a second to check his hair in the reflection of the shiny pipe. Then he pulled out his SpyPad and scanned the area for explosives.

If BIG planned to blow up the mountain, they would already have their dynamite charges in place.

The SpyPad locked onto three bombs. They were attached to the pumping station's main pipe – well spread out to cause the most damage.

Zac would be nabbed for sure if he tried to defuse the dynamite right now. It was more important to make sure the BIG guards were kept out of the way.

Belly Buster time! Zac grinned.

Zac crept along on all fours. He snatched up a hard hat and some oil-stained overalls that were hanging nearby. The overalls were three sizes too big, but they would be a handy disguise if no-one looked too closely.

Zac followed his nose toward the smell of simmering 'omelette surprise'. At the end of the tunnel he peeped through a window into the canteen.

Captain Stewart and the rest of the BIG bruisers were seated at long tables. They were busy chatting and guzzling down cups of coffee.

The cook brought out a tray heaped with butter dishes and toast. This was just the distraction Zac needed!

No-one noticed Zac as he tugged the hard hat low over his face and dashed into the kitchen. The room was empty. On the stove was an enormous frypan with a huge, greasy omelette sizzling away.

Zac crumbled all of the Belly Buster berries into the frypan. He flipped the omelette over and then tip-toed back out into the exit tunnel.

He tossed away the hard hat and was busy pulling off the overalls when a heavy hand latched onto his shoulder.

'Lost your way, Power?'

Zac spun around and found himself face-to-face with Captain Stewart and a pair of scowling guards.

CHAPTER ... ... NINE

'Grab this GIB pest before I strangle him!' growled Captain Stewart, pushing Zac into the waiting arms of the guards. 'Take him to the main cavern.'

Then she spun around and yelled, 'The rest of you, finish morning tea and get back to work – quickly!'

Zac was marched off. In no time he was back on a walkway above the lake. The guards shoved him up against a railing and hand-cuffed his wrists to it.

'Any chance I could get some toast?' asked Zac cheekily. At least they hadn't caught him spiking the omelette.

'Don't push your luck, Power!' snapped Captain Stewart, rubbing a pink scar on her forehead.

That scar must be from the last time we met, thought Zac.

'I can't believe you made it past the Cocka-2s and Arachnotiles, and sneaked into my pumping station!' continued Stewart.

'*Your* pumping station?' asked Zac in disbelief. 'The water inside this mountain belongs to everybody.'

'And *everybody* would've enjoyed it if you'd just paid the ransom,' said Stewart with a nasty cackle. 'But since GIB have sent you, I'm guessing there won't be any ransom. Am I right?'

Captain Stewart didn't wait for an answer. 'You can join the others in the canteen,' she said, calling out to the four guards who had missed out on morning tea. 'Get some food before we leave. Power isn't going anywhere – just yet!'

Stewart moved to a nearby computer and began tapping the keyboard.

'Just to make sure,' she said, with an evil chuckle, 'I'll reprogram a couple of Arachnotile brain control chips for guard duty. Between the two of them they'll keep sixteen eyes on you.'

Two of the scaly terrors slithered from their hiding place inside the rock walls. Fangs bared, they crept toward Zac.

'Any sudden movements and these creatures will get morning tea as well,' said Captain Stewart, glaring at him. 'And Zac Power will be on the menu!'

Stewart opened a metal briefcase and took out an electronic control. She checked it carefully and then locked it back inside the briefcase.

'If GIB aren't delivering that ransom,' she said, ' then I'm getting out of here. I'll blow up the mountain with a remote detonator.'

'But the entire country will be left at the mercy of a drought!' cried Zac, straining against the handcuffs. 'And – '

'And I'll be happily back at BIG's Central Base, sipping a refreshing drink,' said Captain Stewart, cutting him off. 'And I'm leaving you behind, inside this exploding mountain, just like you left me behind inside that exploding submarine! Fitting, don't you think? Now, I'm going to make certain that you haven't meddled with my dynamite.'

She strode off to inspect the charges, taking the detonator briefcase with her.

As soon as she was out of sight, Zac s-l-o-w-l-y began to twist. He eased his

SpyPad out of his back pocket with a couple of fingers. The Arachnotiles hissed but didn't strike. Zac looked over his shoulder at his watch.

Time was running out. Zac had to get the handcuffs off.

He fumbled with the SpyPad and set it to Laser. He knew could easily cut through the handcuffs, but not before the Arachnotiles would reach him.

Unless…

Zac looked for a shiny surface that he could bounce a laser off. Behind his back he got the angle of the SpyPad just right. He lined up his shot on one of the huge shiny pipes.

It was easy enough to get the angle right after all the practice he had playing billiards with Leon every weekend.

Keeping one eye on the Arachnotiles, Zac activated the SpyPad with his pinkie finger. In a bright flash of light, the laser sliced across the pumping station and back again in an instant. At first Zac thought he had missed his target.

Then he saw the smoking holes – he had managed to zap the Arachnotiles!

The monsters quivered, and flopped onto the walkway.

Zac turned the SpyPad laser on the handcuffs. It cut quickly through the metal and Zac shook the handcuffs loose. Without stopping he disappeared behind a huge pump bolted into the rocks.

The fried Arachnotiles rolled off the side of the walkway and splashed into the water below.

Captain Stewart heard the splash and whipped around. She looked up and saw the empty handcuffs dangling from the railing, and her prisoner gone! Roaring with anger, she pounded her fist on an alarm button.

Red alert lights flickered all over the pumping station. She expected the guards to come running but instead —

'Out of the way!' shrieked a BIG guard. 'Coming through! Toilet EMERGENCY!'

Zac peeked out from behind the pump. A group of BIG guards were staggering out of the canteen tunnel onto the walkway. The guards were all bent double, clutching their stomachs. The rest of the guards followed quickly behind, moaning and looking green.

The Belly Buster berries had gone to work – fast!

CHAPTER... ...TEN

'What's wrong with you clowns?' screamed Captain Stewart at the guards. 'Find Power before he ruins everything!'

The guards grumbled and whimpered but they could barely move.

Confused guards stumbled around in all directions. They slouched in tummy agony, faces screwed up and twitching.

'That's it!' growled Captain Stewart, walking swiftly towards an exit. 'In five minutes I can be out the emergency escape tunnel. I'm using the remote detonator on the dynamite as soon as I'm at a safe distance. You're all so useless, you can just take care of yourselves!'

Suddenly Zac had an idea. He hated to do it but he couldn't see any way around it. Zac couldn't risk Captain Stewart blowing up the pipes. And if she was cruel enough to leave her own people behind, maybe she deserved it...

Zac pulled out his iPod. Clutching it in his hand, he sprinted from his hiding place, moving closer to his target.

'There, he is!' shouted Stewart, pointing at Zac running at top speed towards her. 'Get him!'

Zac raised his iPod and hurled it like a frisbee directly at Captain Stewart.

CRUUUUUUNCH!

The iPod struck her right on the forehead in exactly the same spot as last time. Captain Stewart slumped to the walkway, passed out cold. She dropped the remote detonator briefcase as she fell.

Zac kicked it into the lake. It sank, leaving a trail of bubbles.

Maybe a flying iPod isn't such a bad weapon after all! thought Zac.

The BIG guards didn't look like they'd cause any trouble. Most of them had slowed to a standstill, their aching stomachs gurgling loudly.

There was only 20 minutes left, and still one *deadly* detail.

Zac ran over to the first of the explosive charges. The BIG bombs were very complex and *very* powerful. Each one had enough bang to punch a hole in Craggy Mountain the size of a skyscraper.

If these charges went off, the pumping station would be totally destroyed, and the secret mountain lake would leak out in a matter of seconds.

There was no way Zac could work out how to disarm them without a top-level two-week course at the GIB Spy Academy. The timers were still ticking away, set for a noon detonation.

Zac felt around in his pocket for Leon's Fizzle-44 Explosion Inhibitor.

Zac tugged out the retractable lead and fastened the mini-nozzle onto the nearest bomb. He tapped the 'on' button. The LCD screen flashed on.

INHIBITOR ACTIVATED

Bombs detected: 3

Time to disarm: 24 mins

The Fizzle-44 was a great idea but Leon must have designed it for much smaller bombs! Zac quickly did the maths in his head. The Inhibitor would be four minutes too slow! At noon he'd be going back down Craggy Mountain – in a thousand pieces!

He needed to give the Fizzle-44 a power boost. *But how?*

Zac slapped his forehead as he realised the answer. All he had to do was turn on the turbine pumps and open the giant water release valves!

If he got the water flowing through the pipes right now, he could link the Fizzle-44 to the pumping station's mighty turbines with his SpyPad. That would be all the power boost it needed!

Zac scrolled down Leon's mission documents on his SpyPad. He found the blueprints for the pumping station and went to work finding a computer control panel to get the water flowing.

Gotcha!

Zac rushed to the computer. Every second counted. He set his SpyPad to Wireless Network. He linked the computer with the Fizzle-44.

Fingers crossed, he hit 'start'.

The rock walls and walkways began to shake as the turbine engines ground into action and the giant valves opened. The movement increased to a shudder like an earthquake. Millions of gigalitres of water began to gush through the Craggy Mountain pipes and start the long journey across the country.

Zac made it back to the Fizzle-44 just in time to see the LCD screen display the words: Operation complete!

The dynamite was defused and the water was surging through the pipes.

Zac used the SpyPad's satellite phone to call the Aqua Glide.

'Agent Rock Star reporting in,' he said. 'The water is flowing – mission successful. I even have a few minutes to spare!'

'Zac, it's Leon,' came his brother's voice. 'I'm relieved you made it OK. We were getting worried.'

'Can you please organise an arrest team?' asked Zac, looking around at the sick and sorry BIG guards. 'I could do with a hand to carry out the bad guys.'

'Sure thing,' said Leon. 'I'll send a flight of rescue choppers from GIB Headquarters now. They'll be there shortly.'

Zac's stomach rumbled, and he realised how hungry he was. He couldn't wait to get back to Mama's Pizza Palace!

'Hey Zac,' Leon added, 'before I sign off, I've received a message for you from Agent Tool Belt.'

'Oh yeah? What did Dad say?' asked Zac.

Leon paused. 'He said to remind you you're on bathroom duty tonight – and you'd better clean it before the pipes burst!' he blurted out with a laugh.

Your mission: read all the books
in the Zac Power series ...

END

READING
>>> ON

MISSION CHECKLIST
How many have you read?

POISON ISLAND

DEEP WATERS

MIND GAMES 3

FROZEN FEAR 4

TOMB OF DOOM 5

SHOCKWAVE 10

BOOT CAMP 15

SHIPWRECK 20